The Berenstain Bears' EASTER CLASSICS

Stan & Jan Berenstain

Random House  New York

Published in the United States by Random House Children's Books,
a division of Penguin Random House LLC, New York.
The stories in this collection were
originally published separately in the United States
by Random House Children's Books in 1999 and 2002.

2019 Random House Children's Books Edition
Random House and the colophon
are registered trademarks of Penguin Random House LLC.

Visit us on the Web!
rhcbooks.com
BerenstainBears.com

Educators and librarians, for a variety of teaching tools,
visit us at RHTeachersLibrarians.com

ISBN: 978-0-525-64756-0

Printed in the United States of America 10 9 8 7 6 5 4 3 2

Random House Children's Books supports the First Amendment
and celebrates the right to read.

Contents

The Berenstain Bears

and the Big Question

Many cubs' questions
strike grownups as odd,
but the really big one
is "Mama, what's God?"

Early one weekend morning, Sister Bear was busy having a tea party with her dolls. She poured the tea into each of the dolls' cups. It was really apple juice. Sister didn't much care for tea. She served cookies, too.

"You're welcome, my dears," Sister said, pretending that the dolls had thanked her.

"Now," she said, folding her hands, "let's say grace."

The Bear family usually said grace before meals. Sometimes they were in such a hurry or so hungry that they forgot . . . especially Papa. But Mama usually reminded them.

So Sister bowed her head, closed her eyes, and said:

Thank you for the world so sweet.
Thank you for the food we eat.
Thank you for the birds that sing.
Thank you, God, for everything.

Then Sister drank her juice and ate her cookies. The dolls weren't very hungry, so Sister drank their juice and ate their cookies, too.

Later, when Sister and Mama were washing up the tea things, Sister grew thoughtful. "Mama," she said, a faraway look in her eyes, "what's God?"

Papa and Brother were just coming in from having a catch, and Papa overheard Sister's question. "That's a very Big Question, Sister," he interrupted before Mama could say anything. "It happens to be a question that people have been asking for a very long time."

Taking Sister by the hand, he led her into the living room and sat her on his knee. "Now," he said, "let me see if I can explain it to you." And then Papa began to give Sister a BIG, BORING LECTURE.

Mama decided to step in. "That's all very interesting, Papa," she said, taking Sister off his knee. "But if you'll excuse us, Sister and I have some gardening to do."

Mama took Sister outside into the garden. It was a beautiful morning. The sun was shining, the birds were singing, and the flowers were all in bloom. “Now, Sister,” Mama said as she began weeding her garden, “all you need to remember is that God made everything—the birds, the flowers, the sunshine. They’re all God’s work—all part of God’s Great Plan.”

Sister looked around at the wide, beautiful world and thought it over. "You mean," she said, "God made *everything*—everything in the whole wide world?"

"That's right, dear," said Mama.

"Did He make clouds and trees and butterflies?" asked Sister.

"Of course," answered Mama. "Everything."

But Sister didn't stop there. "Did He make worms and spiders and big yellow slugs?" she asked.

“Yes,” nodded Mama, feeling a little sick as she picked a big yellow slug off her favorite geraniums. “As I said, they’re all part of God’s Great Plan.”

"What about bellyaches?" Sister went on. "What about cold germs? What about earthquakes, floods, fires, and tornadoes?"

"Hmm!" said Mama, rubbing her chin thoughtfully. "This is an even Bigger Question than I realized!"

"Look!" said Sister, pointing to the road nearby. "There's Gramps and Gran—and they're all dressed up!"

"That's because they're wearing their Sunday-go-to-meeting clothes," said Mama.

"Good morning," said Gran. "We're going to services at the chapel in the woods. Why don't you join us?"

"Hmm," said Mama. "Why don't we, indeed?" Then she marched inside, got her purse, and put on her hat.

"Where are you going?" wondered Papa, noticing her getting ready to go out.

"*We,*" answered Mama firmly, "are all going to services at the chapel in the woods."

"Services?" said Brother as she led him down the front steps. "What's that?"

“That,” explained Papa,
hurrying after them, “is where
we bears go when we want to
think about Big Questions.”

It was quiet and peaceful in the chapel—and very pretty, too. The sun shone in through windows made of bits of colored glass. Dust sparkles floated in the rays of light. An organ began to play. "Look," said Brother. "That's old Widder McGrizz playing the organ."

"Shhh!" said Mama. "The preacher's about to speak."

"Welcome, friends," said the preacher. "I'm glad to see you all here this morning. I'm especially glad to see visitors who haven't been with us before." Sister and Brother sat up. The preacher was talking about *them*.

"Now, I know you're all expecting to hear me preach," he went on. "That's why they call me the preacher." There were a few chuckles.

"But this morning," he said, "we're going to do things a little differently. Instead of me doin' the preachin', I want you to do it." The bears, all seated on long benches, looked at each other. "That's right," he said. "You do the preachin' today. Just sit there and think about the big questions of life, and when the spirit moves you, stand up and speak your piece."

It grew very still and quiet. The bench was very hard, and Sister had an itch right between her shoulder blades. But before it got too bad, someone stood up and started to speak.

It was Farmer Ben. “On this fine spring morning,” he said, “I’ve been thinking about our beautiful Bear Country—about its woods and fields, its sparkling streams and rolling hills. I’m thankful for Bear Country. I feel thankful to God for giving us such a beautiful land in which to live.” And he sat down.

The itch between Sister's shoulder blades had gone away. But now she noticed a fly crawling on the back of the bench in front of her. She wanted to swat at it. But she was afraid to make a commotion. Luckily, someone else stood up to speak.

It was Grizzly Gran. "I, too, am thankful—to see my grandcubs, Brother and Sister, here with me this morning. I feel thankful to God for two such wonderful cubs." And she sat down.

Brother and Sister felt a little embarrassed. They knew that Gramps and Gran loved them. But it had never occurred to them that their grandparents might thank God for them! Before they could feel too embarrassed, Mama was standing up to speak. “It’s been a long time since I’ve been here,” she said. “I guess we’ve just been too busy with everyday things. But I’m glad we came this morning. It helps me think things through.” And she sat down.

The gathering lasted a little longer. Sister had a few more itches. A few more bears stood up to speak. But then it was all over, and everyone was shaking hands and talking and filing out.

The Bear family waved good-bye to Gramps and Gran and headed down the road to their tree house. Papa Bear hoisted Sister up on his shoulders to give her a ride, and Brother ran ahead, doing cartwheels to get the kinks out after sitting still for so long.

Sister Bear looked up at the clouds in the deep blue sky and at the swallows swooping overhead and sighed. “Mama,” she said.

“Yes, dear?” asked Mama.

“What about questions?” Sister asked.

“Questions?” said Mama.

"Yes, questions," Sister repeated. "Did God make questions?"

"Yes, Sister," Papa answered as they came to the top of a hill and looked out over their tree house home nestled in a beautiful valley in Bear Country. "*Mostly* questions."

The Berenstain Bears

and the REAL EASTER EGGS

To celebrate new life at Easter,
eggs and bunnies come in handy.
But some cubs think
it's just about candy.

"Nineteen . . . twenty . . . twenty-one . . . twenty-two . . . twenty-three. How about that?" said Sister Bear. "I got twenty-three valentines at school today—seven signed with names, eight guess-whos, and eight SWAKs."

Brother smiled. He knew that there were twenty-four cubs in Sister's class and Teacher Jane made every cub give every other cub a valentine.

But Sister was enjoying her valentines so much that he didn't say anything. Besides, he'd gotten quite a few himself.

"I just *love* holidays!" said Sister. "I wish every day was a holiday. Then you could get stuff every day."

"Oh?" said Mama, who'd been listening. "Is that all holidays mean to you—getting stuff?"

"Sure," said Sister. "You get turkey, stuffing, and pumpkin pie on Thanksgiving, presents on Christmas, and valentines on Valentine's Day. What's wrong with that?"

"What's *wrong* with that," said Mama, "is that holidays are about much more. Thanksgiving is about being thankful, Christmas is about good will and peace on earth, and Valentine's Day is about love and friendship."

"What do you think about that, my dear?" asked Papa. "Er, where did Sister go?" he said, looking around.

"She went into the kitchen," said Brother.

Which Sister had.

She'd gone into the kitchen to look at the calendar on the wall. She was looking ahead for holidays. She looked at the rest of February. There weren't any more big holidays in February.

She looked at March. She didn't see any big holidays in March either.

But then she looked at April, and right there in April was a really big holiday: *Easter! Yum!* she thought. *Coconut eggs, jellybeans, chocolate bunnies! Yum! And double yum!*

That night, Sister fell asleep while visions of jellybeans and chocolate bunnies danced in her head.

But it was still winter, and when she woke up the next morning she forgot about Easter and spring because there was a new blanket of snow covering the earth—

wonderful snow to sled on,

to make forts out of,

to make angel wings in.

But Mother Nature hadn't forgotten.

And while Brother, Sister, and their friends sledded and made forts and angel wings, she was getting ready for a whole new season.

As the winter winds died down and the sun began to ride higher in the sky, signs of spring began to appear.

The big icicles of winter dropped from roofs and stuck like swords in the last of the melting snow.

Robins began looking for places to build their nests.

Blue and yellow crocuses peeped through the softening earth.

And it wasn't very long before reminders of Easter began to appear in supermarkets . . .

and on television.

But it was the big billboard in the town square that got Sister and Brother really excited about Easter.

This is what it said:

"Look," said Brother. "It says the prizes are on display in the window of the Beartown General Store."

And were they ever!

There were more jellybeans than you could ever count; sugar-trimmed, dark-chocolate, coconut-filled eggs with sugar roses and violets on them; life-sized, milk-chocolate bunnies; and one chocolate bunny as big as Brother Bear himself.

Happy Easter, indeed! This was going to be the biggest, best, most delicious Easter ever.

Brother and Sister were so excited they ran all the way home.

Mama was in the tree house front yard.

"Sister," said Brother, "you tell Mama about the big Easter egg hunt while I go find Papa and tell him."

"Mama! Mama!" sputtered Sister. She was so excited and out of breath she could hardly talk.

"Now, my dear," said Mama, "I know that what you want to tell me is very exciting, but I'm sure it can wait until you catch your breath. Meanwhile, I've got some exciting things to show you."

"But, Mama!" protested Sister.

"Just look here," said Mama, kneeling down. "See these little blue and yellow flowers? They're from the crocus bulbs I planted last fall. They've been sleeping under the snow all winter. Now they're the first to push up through the earth and greet the spring. Aren't they lovely?"

"Yes, Mama, they're nice," said Sister. "But Brother and I were just down at the town square and guess what?"

But Mama didn't quite hear Sister because she had walked across the yard and was looking closely at a scratchy-looking bush. It didn't look like much to Sister.

"This is a forsythia," said Mama. "It doesn't look like much now, but come the first warm, sunny day it will burst with thousands of brilliant yellow flowers. Surely you remember it from last spring, my dear?"

Sister did, sort of. And it *was* pretty. But it didn't begin to compare with those sugar roses and violets on those dark-chocolate Easter eggs, or those zillions of brightly colored jellybeans.

That's when Papa and Brother came running around the house. Papa was just as excited as Brother and Sister.

"How about that?" cried Papa.
"How about what?" said Mama.
"Didn't Sister tell you?" said Papa. "There's going to be a big Easter egg hunt on the town square and you should hear the prizes—more jellybeans than you could ever count—"

“Papa?” said Brother.

“All kinds of chocolate eggs!” continued Papa.

“Papa?” repeated Brother, tugging on Papa’s pant leg.

“Er, yes, son?”

“I forgot to tell you,” said Brother. “The Easter egg hunt is just for cubs.”

“Just for cubs?” said Papa.
“That’s right,” said Brother.
“Oh,” said Papa. He was more than a little disappointed. Papa was crazy about jellybeans—especially the black ones.

Mama sighed. She looked at Papa and the cubs. She was a little disappointed, too.

The day of the Easter egg hunt dawned bright and early. Sister, Brother, and dozens of their friends were on the town square waiting for Mayor Honeypot to give the signal for the hunt to begin. They had bags and baskets of every shape to gather the eggs. Brother and Sister were especially well prepared. They each had a big basket—the better to carry the eggs they would find.

When the mayor gave the signal, it was helter-skelter, gather-gather—here an egg, there an egg, everywhere an egg-egg. But Brother and Sister had a plan. Instead of hunting where the other cubs were, they quickly moved to the woods at the edge of the square.

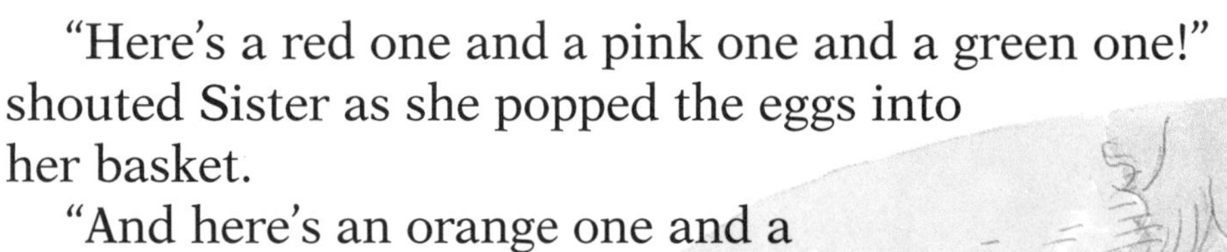

“Here’s a red one and a pink one and a green one!” shouted Sister as she popped the eggs into her basket.

“And here’s an orange one and a yellow one and a lavender one!” cried Brother as he popped them into his basket.

A little while later, Brother noticed that Sister had become very quiet.

He turned and saw her standing ever so still, looking into some bushes.

"And here," said Sister in a soft, hushed voice that Brother could hardly hear, "are five tiny blue eggs in a nest deep in the bushes." Ever so carefully and quietly, Brother moved into the bushes and looked over Sister's shoulder at *the real Easter eggs*.

And together they watched as, one by one, each tiny blue egg cracked open and a tiny, scraggly, wet baby robin struggled to climb out. From time to time, the mother or father robin came to the nest with food—worms and insects. They took turns putting the food in the wide-open beaks of the baby birds.

Brother and Sister watched for a long time. They hardly moved. It was as if they were under a spell. It was the most wonderful and amazing thing they had ever seen.

They missed most of the Easter egg hunt. But since every cub got a prize, they got some goodies for the eggs they had already gathered—a few chocolate eggs, but mostly jellybeans, which they shared with Papa. They gave him the black ones.

Many of Sister and Brother's friends won the really big prizes. But that was okay. The sugar-trimmed chocolate eggs and the giant chocolate bunny would not only soon be gone, they would leave quite a few tummy aches behind.

EASTER EGG HUNT
HEADQUARTERS

Sister and Brother would never forget those baby birds. And the wonder of Easter and its message of new life would stay with them forever.